TALES OF VIRTUE FOR ANIMALS AND MAN

ROGER BELTZ

PREFACE

Five short stories, works of allegorical fiction, are contained in this book. It is hoped the reader will find these to be entertaining and thought provoking at the same time. And while the stories are fictitious, there is one bedrock truth I hope you will find in this book. God exists, He loves you, and He wants a relationship with you. You can find that truth expressed in a wonderful book titled, *The Holy Bible.*

Many thanks to my two editors, Pam and Debra. One was paid, and the other was not. But both spent time not just correcting my errors, but also giving advice on the story line.

elissa Sue Erinbright was a young pig who lived in the town of Millenberg by Millenberg Lake. She lived in a nice house with her two loving parents and five siblings. She and the other young animals in the town attended Millenberg School which had grades one through twelve.

Even before she was able to talk, Melissa Sue gave her vocal chords a daily workout. As a baby she would cry for hours at a time unless her parents gave her their constant attention. When she was able to speak, which came for her at an early age, the crying stopped, but the almost incessant talking began.

But it wasn't the talking which made Melissa Sue a problem; it was what she talked about. Once, as a young child in church while the pastor was giving his sermon, Melissa Sue asked so loudly even Mr. Johnson who had forgotten his hearing aid that day could hear, "Mommy, Cindy told me Little Stevey still wets his bed. Do you think his parents beat him?"

Mrs. Erinbright, her face bright red with embarrassment,

had to get up, and with her daughter in tow, exit the church service. All the way down the aisle, the other parishioners could hear the still clueless Melissa Sue asking, "Mommy, do you think they are bad parents? I think they must be."

Once out of the church service, Mrs. Erinbright, as she had done several times before, told Melissa Sue it was not appropriate to talk during the sermon. And then she told her, "Melissa, it is not right to talk about others that way. That is gossip. Even if it is true that Stevey still wets the bed, you should never repeat that. It could embarrass him."

"But Cindy told me," replied Melissa Sue. "Why was it okay for her to say it?"

"It isn't okay for her to say it. She is gossiping too. And talking about his parents is gossip also, terrible gossip. Wherever did you come up with such an idea about them?" her mother asked.

Melissa Sue looked around and shifted uncomfortably. "Maybe Cindy and I talked about it."

"Maybe you need to not spend time with Cindy if you are going to talk about others that way. Your father and I will talk about this after church," her mother said sternly.

Her parents did talk about it and decided on a punishment. They also talked again with Melissa Sue about gossip and why it is wrong and bad to do.

Some years went by, and although her parents were aware she kept gossiping, she didn't seem to do it as often, and there didn't seem to be any big stories which hurt others. Yes, there was the time she told everyone Johnny Squirrel had cheated on a test because he looked in the direction of Freddy Toad. But Johnny had gotten an A on the test while Freddy had flunked it. So there was no damage done. And, of course, there was the time she told everyone Mrs. Treat, the math teacher, was having an affair with Mr. Peterson, the PE teacher. That resulted in a conference at the principal's office where it was explained to Melissa Sue that Mr. Peterson had moved out of the area to take a job at another school before Mrs. Treat started as a teacher at Millenberg. That did result in some embarrassment for Mrs. Treat. And Melissa Sue's parents had to apologize for that.

While her parents were happy there were no big incidents, the students and teachers considered Melissa Sue to be a gossip. In fact, her nickname was Missy the Mouth. With a reputation like that it was difficult for her to make friends. But one day, Becky, who had just moved there, started coming to school. Melissa Sue and Becky sat next to each other in class and talked. Melissa Sue was anxious to become her friend and went with her to lunch.

Becky shared how she happened to come to Millenberg. "My parents are so stupid. My father lost his job in the city. This was the only place he could find a job. I had to leave all my friends. Can you believe it? I mean, well you probably have great parents."

Melissa Sue, wanting desperately to be friends with Becky, said what she thought she should in order to be Becky's friend. "Oh no, I think I understand. My parents are not very smart either. I mean, they bought a vacation house they couldn't afford."

"Oh, that must have been so embarrassing. What happened?" Becky whispered.

Melissa Sue thought about what would sound the best to Becky. "Well, they couldn't make the payments. How stupid is that? And then the bank took the house back."

Becky smiled. "Wow, you're right. Your parents really blew it."

Melissa Sue smiled also and then went home that day with a warm feeling in her heart. And the next day she went to school anxious to meet with her new friend and to share more secrets.

But when she and her siblings got to school things were not as she had expected. All the kids were pointing at her and laughing and smirking and saying, "Missy the Mouth lost her house. Now she has no place to stay."

When she got to class the girl next to her said loudly, "Melissa Sue, if you need a place to live you can stay in our backyard." Then she and all the kids around her laughed while Melissa Sue turned red and hid her face.

During lunch Melissa Sue found Becky sitting with some other kids. Melissa Sue confronted her. "How could you tell everyone what I told you? That was terrible. And what about your parents? You said your dad lost his job and that you had to come here because this was the only place he could find a job."

Becky looked at her and spoke so all the kids around her could hear. "I told you a story because my friends told me you are a gossip. As for my parents, they have millions of dollars. They retired early and moved here to enjoy life."

Then Becky and all the other young animals laughed at Melissa Sue as she ran from the cafeteria and all the way back home. She tried to sneak into the house, but her mother was home and saw her. "What are you doing home from school so early?"

"I didn't feel well at lunch so I came home," replied Melissa Sue doing her best to look sick.

"Dear, you should have let a teacher know and then they would have called your dad and me," her mother said as she held her daughter. "One of us would have come to get you. What's the matter? You don't seem to have a fever."

"I am just sick to my stomach, that's all. I wanted to throw up," answered Melissa Sue.

"Why don't you go to bed and see if you can sleep. I'll check up on you a little later," said her mother.

"Thank you, Mom," Melissa Sue said as she gave her a

hug. Then she went up the stairs to her room and went to sleep. Sometime later she awoke. It was dark outside. She could hear her father yelling.

"Everyone thinks we are going broke because of her. She opened her big mouth and made up a story, and now everyone thinks we have no money." Then her father yelled up the stairs, "Melissa Sue, get down here now. We need to talk."

She got dressed and opened the door to her room. Her brothers and sisters were all staring at her with angry faces. Then she figured out what had happened. When they got home from school they had squealed to their mom about what she did, and their dad had just gotten home and been told about it.

Melissa Sue went downstairs and met with her very angry father and her concerned mother. They told her they bought a house for her grandma so she could live close by. But she died before she could move in. So, of course they did not keep that house. Then her father yelled at her and asked her how she could say such terrible things about them. He told her even if they had been forced to give a house back to the bank that she should never have told anyone about it.

Melissa Sue was grounded for the next month which really did not bother her as none of the kids were even friendly to her. The worst thing for her was having to go to school. But as time passed the memory of that event faded in the minds of the young students and, as so often happens, new events replaced the old. Once again things returned to normal for Melissa Sue.

Then one day, in her junior year, she fell in with a group of three other girls who loved to gossip. They didn't care what others thought of them. All the other students and many of the teachers feared them. They knew things about others. That knowledge was power which they knew how to use.

Then it hit Melissa Sue. Gossiping wasn't a problem. It was not knowing how to gossip properly that was a problem. All those years she had gossiped but she didn't know how to really use it. Now she would learn how to use it. This gave her a sense of power which made her feel very warm and happy on the inside.

On that day she sang this little song,

> *"Gossip is such a tasty treat.*
> *Its power is sublime.*
> *In all my days with little heat,*
> *Keeps me warm a lifetime.*
>
> *Gossip is a friend you can't beat.*
> *She's always there in time.*
> *Tells me I'm very smart and neat,*
> *So very, very prime!"*

So she enjoyed her last two years of high school with her three friends. And though her parents knew she kept gossiping, and they did not approve of her friendship with those three girls, they left her alone because she did not gossip about them.

Once she graduated her friends went their own ways, and Melissa Sue was left by herself. As was common in Millenberg, many of the graduates went right to work instead of going to college. Melissa Sue was able to get an office job at a local business where they didn't know about her habit of gossiping.

She quickly became friends with Chloe, a fellow employee who had been there for a year. One day they went out to lunch. Melissa Sue learned Chloe had a hard time with the boss, Mr. Royce, when she first started there. "That big fat pig, no offense meant," she said, looking at Melissa Sue. "He said I was talking on the phone too much. I had a sick kid. What was I supposed to do? I had to make sure he was okay. And there he sat in his office talking on the phone. I know he was making personal phone calls. He still does it. We have to work while he gets to play. It's just unfair."

"I do see him on the phone a lot," said Melissa Sue. "Maybe he is talking to his girlfriend, though I don't know who would want to go out with him."

The two giggled and quickly finished their lunch before returning to the office. Melissa Sue set about doing her work. She was startled when Chloe came up to her, tears in her eyes. "Mr. Royce fired me."

Melissa's eyes grew big. "Why?"

"It was that stupid rabbit, Mr. Pearls, with those big ears. He's a spy for Mr. Royce. He overheard us at lunch." And with that, Chloe was ushered out of the office.

Just then Mr. Pearls came up to Melissa Sue. He grinned. "Mr. Royce wants to see you. Now."

Melissa Sue went into Mr. Royce's office with a sick feeling in her stomach.

"Have a seat, Miss Erinbright," ordered Mr. Royce. "I'll make this quick. This is your first and last warning. I don't tolerate gossip, especially gossip about me. You're new here so I'm giving you a break. But if I catch you doing it again, I'll fire you. And as for your information, I am happily married. Now you can get out of my office."

Melissa Sue was very sad that day. She had just lost a friend, and had almost been fired. She stopped by the lake after work and started throwing rocks in the water and talking to herself. "I can't believe it. This is such a horrible day. I was doing so well. I made a friend and now my friend is gone. I'm so lonely."

"Are you okay?" came a gentle voice full of concern.

Melissa Sue jumped and looked around. "Who's there?"

"It's better if you don't know who I am right now. You'll be scared if you see me. Really, I'm just concerned that you're okay," said the soft voice.

Melissa Sue looked over at some bushes by the water. "Come out of the bushes. Show yourself."

"It would be better if you could get to know me a little better first," said the voice. "I don't want to scare you. I could use a friend, and it sounds like you could use one as well. You know, I am often misunderstood. That's why so many animals don't like me. I bet you are misunderstood also."

Melissa Sue pouted and talked to the voice in the bushes being careful to not get too close. "Yes, I am greatly misunderstood. All my life I've been misunderstood and so few of my fellow animals have ever liked me. Then my best friend got fired today, and I almost got fired."

"That sounds terrible. And you seem so nice," said the voice.

"Well, you're very nice to say so. All I did today was tell the truth in a private conversation. My boss takes private calls at work but gets mad when others take private calls," said Melissa Sue. "Oh no, I shouldn't have said that. If my boss finds out he'll fire me. You're not a spy for my boss are you? That's how I got in trouble today, a big fat furry spy with big ears. Oh no, how do I know you're not a spy?"

"Please don't be afraid. I'm not a spy. Here, I will show you myself. But please don't be afraid. All my life I've been misunderstood just like you. But I will show you myself. Then you will know I'm not a spy. And I will not leave the water. You know you are safe when I am in the water," said the voice.

Then a shadow out in the water moved from behind the

bushes and two yellow eyes with black slits in them appeared. And then the rest of its head appeared.

"Why, you're an alligator," cried Melissa Sue. "I can't talk to you. You'll try to eat me."

"Please don't say that. Everyone says that. And all I want is a friend. I just want someone to talk with, to share stories with. But everyone thinks I am horrible," cried the alligator. "I guess I will have to go somewhere else. My name is Agatha, by the way. Well, goodbye. Nice to meet you."

Melissa Sue wasn't sure if it was the plaintive voice of the alligator or her own loneliness, but something stirred inside of her. "No, wait. I'll talk with you, only you must stay in the water."

"Oh, thank you. You are so kind. No one has ever been so kind to me," replied Agatha.

And so the two talked for awhile longer, until Melissa Sue thought it was time for her to go. But the two agreed to meet again at the same time in a few weeks.

At their next meeting, Melissa Sue decided to tell Agatha about Mr. Pearls. "He's a big fat rabbit with huge ears. Why, if he weren't so fat those ears would make him fall over on his big pink nose.

"He sounds so mean. I bet he is rich and has a nice house while so many others don't have nice houses," said Agatha.

"Yes, he is rich. He might even be richer than Mr. Royce. His parents left him money and a mansion down by the lake. It has two towers on it which were built to look like rabbit ears. He lives in that huge house all by himself. Oh, and he has a big garden. He always brags about his huge garden. He says he goes out every day after work to pick the vegetables in his garden. Can you believe it? He thinks he's too good to use the store," said Melissa Sue.

"Well, he does sound terrible," said Agatha. "It just doesn't seem right."

Melissa Sue went home that day singing her song,

> *"Gossip is such a tasty treat.*
> *Its power is sublime.*
> *In all my days with little heat,*
> *Keeps me warm a lifetime.*
> *Gossip is a friend you can't beat.*
> *She's always there in time.*
> *Tells me I'm very smart and neat,*
> *So very, very prime!"*

Some days later at work Mr. Royce held a meeting. "I'm sorry to inform you Mr. Pearls is missing. We don't know what happened to him. Maybe he had to go visit a sick relative. Maybe it was an emergency so he didn't have time to let anyone know. The police are looking into it."

Melissa Sue couldn't wait to see Agatha again. Mr. Pearls having disappeared without telling anyone was good news. He would be in trouble. And then there would be no spy for Mr. Royce.

At their next meeting, Melissa Sue found Agatha on the beach. She was startled. "Agatha, what are you doing out of the water?"

"Oh please, don't make me get back in the lake," Agatha said softly. "I get so cold in there. I'm not like you. I have to have sunshine to warm up."

"I guess it's okay. No, I'm sure it's okay. But please don't mind if I don't get too close," said Melissa Sue. "Oh, I have to tell you about Mr. Pearls. He took off without telling anyone where he had gone. He will be in so much trouble when he gets back. And you should see Mr. Royce. He's all torn up about it. We all know it's just because his spy is gone. I can't believe it. He is such a fake. Do you know he wears a hair piece? He pretends it is his real hair, and he gets mad if anyone says otherwise. He's another one with a huge house on the lake, a huge gold-colored house. He says it's that color because he is so rich. Who would be so stupid to paint their house all in gold? Oh, and every Saturday morning, he goes down to his own private dock and sits in a recliner and drinks tea. He says he soaks up the rays and that it makes him stay young."

Melissa Sue just kept talking and talking with Agatha content to just listen.

The next Monday when Melissa Sue went in to work there was Mr. Royce's boss. He held a meeting with all the employees and told them Mr. Royce was missing and that Mr. Turner would be the acting boss until they could find Mr. Royce.

Melissa Sue was very excited about this news and again could hardly wait until she saw Agatha.

At their next meeting there was Agatha again resting on the bank, but Melissa Sue didn't mind this time. She was so excited to tell Agatha about Mr. Royce having disappeared with no trace. Then she told her about Mr. Turner. "You should see him. He is a small frog. He has to sit on a pillow to be able to see over the top of Mr. Royce's desk. How in the world can he do the job?"

"Oh, he sounds terribly small, not even worth bothering about," replied Agatha. "But you know, I am ready to tell you my story now, Melissa Sue. We're good enough friends now that I can tell you my story."

This caught Melissa Sue's attention. So few had ever called her their friend. That was very special. "Why of course, I am happy to hear your story, Agatha."

So Agatha began her story. "I was in a large family. My daddy was always mean to me, and my mom didn't care. And I never got to go to school. It was so terrible at home that I left, and I found a job at a factory. I got married and had kids while I was there."

At this point Agatha began to cry a little and her voice got softer. So Melissa Sue took a couple of steps closer.

"I had good ideas to make the factory work better and to make things better for the workers at the same time," said Agatha. "So I shared my ideas with the boss. He said they were great ideas and that he would tell the managers. So I waited and waited. One day they made one of my changes. I was so excited. I went to the boss, but he told me he didn't remember talking to me. I reminded him we had talked. And then, he fired me. Oh, it still hurts to this day."

Agatha's voice continued getting softer, and Melissa Sue kept getting closer to be able to hear. "I went home to my husband. He wasn't able to work. He was hurt badly in an accident. That job was all we had to put food on the table. But then, Melissa Sue, I have to tell you," Agatha whispered as she turned to look in the eyes of Melissa Sue who was now standing right next to her. "You need to know I ate that precious Mr. Pearls and that big Mr. Royce too, but Mr. Turner is way too small, so you will have to do."

And with that Agatha opened her mouth and swallowed Melissa Sue. And as she swam away Agatha could be heard singing,

> *"The fruit of gossip tastes so sweet.*
> *It keeps my belly full.*
> *I do not know what I would eat.*

If gossip weren't so cool."

Melissa Sue knew gossip tastes very good and makes you feel very important. And though she knew it hurt others she didn't care. She never realized until the end that eventually gossip will eat you.

THE UNBEARABLE BURDEN

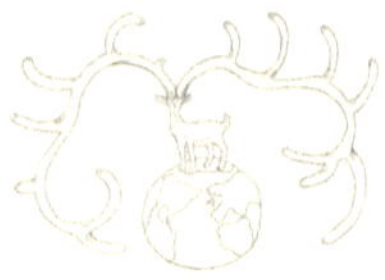

The Brombey Deer were the deer who lived in the Brombey Forest in the Michesney Hills. Life was good for the Brombey Deer with plenty of food and shelter. They were, as a rule, kind and gentle deer, and they had good reputations among all the other forest dwellers. It was into the Brombey Deer that the twin bucks Philippe and Pascal were born some years ago.

As young deer, Philippe and Pascal had a great time together. They always competed to see who was the best. They had contests to see who could leap the farthest, jump the highest, and run the fastest. And in these contests Philippe always won.

But Pascal never became sad when he lost. Instead he would say, "Philippe, you are a wonderful athlete. You will grow up to be a great strong leader."

One day in one of their races, a raccoon mother with some of her babies stepped out onto the trail in front of Philippe. This caused him to fall, but he still won the race.

Philippe snorted. "Can you believe it? That stupid

raccoon stepped out in front of me and made me fall! She should be more careful. I could have been hurt."

"Don't worry about it," said Pascal. "I'm sure she didn't do it on purpose. Besides we have to share the trail with others. Let's go on to see who can leap higher."

Philippe glowered. "All right, but she really should be more careful."

When they became old enough to go to school they both played soccer. Philippe was a very good player. "Look at how good I am Pascal. You are right. I'm the best athlete. But look at what the others do. They are jealous. I was completely open and Bobby Buck refused to pass the ball to me. And Debby Doe kicked the ball into my face. And Daisy Deer tripped me."

"But Philippe," replied Pascal. "Soccer is a rough game. Sometimes we make mistakes and sometimes we do things no good deer should do. Besides Debby and Daisy apologized to you. They are very nice. You know they didn't do it on purpose."

"I don't know about that," said Philippe. "You know deer can apologize to you and not really mean it. And what about Bobby Buck? He didn't say a thing. I know he saw me. He was looking right at me. I could have scored a goal if he had passed the ball to me."

Pascal didn't answer Philippe. He knew his brother would not like the answer. He knew his brother was a very good athlete and sometimes hogged the ball. Bobby Buck had wanted to give someone else a chance to play.

Then the day came that Pascal left the Brombey Forest to study in a foreign land. While Philippe was a gifted athlete, Pascal was a gifted student and had always wanted to study and live in another country. So Pascal went away to school, but Philippe was content to stay in the forest. Yet Pascal did not forget his home and periodically came back to visit.

The first time Pascal came back he went to see his brother. "Philippe, I am back to visit. Let's have a race."

"Okay, Brother, but you are going to lose," replied Philippe as he stood up from where he was resting.

"Wow," said Pascal. "Look at your antlers. An older buck would be happy to have those antlers. You have so many points, and it isn't even the time for antlers yet."

"They are wonderful, aren't they?" answered Philippe.

"Yes, they are very impressive," Pascal replied. "The does must all be crazy about you."

Philippe frowned. "You would think so. But they don't seem to care. I am stronger and faster than any of the other bucks, and my antlers are the best. But it doesn't matter. The does say they want someone who is nicer. They say appearance is not everything."

"Well, I can't believe that," said Pascal. "I know some day you will become a great leader. Come on. Let's get your mind off that and race. The first one to the dead pine tree is the winner."

And so they were off to compete in running, leaping, and jumping. As had happened so many times before, Philippe won easily. But as always, Pascal told him he was a wonderful athlete and that he would be a great leader.

"Oh Pascal, I wish you had not left me. I really have no friends here anymore. The does used to dance with me at the community dances, but now I am lucky if I can get one of the wall flowers to dance with me. And who wants to dance with them? Can you believe the does will dance with Shaky Shivers? You remember him. He was always so scared. He would see his own shadow and think there was a creature behind him ready to eat him. Then he would shoot straight up in the air. That was so funny."

Pascal laughed. "Yes, that was funny. Is he still the same?"

"Yes. That is what I can't believe. The does dance with

him, but not with me. It just isn't right. And then there are the other bucks. They used to invite me to their campouts. But at one of the campouts I got into an argument with Bobby Buck. You remember him. He was the one who wouldn't pass the ball to me in soccer."

Pascal shook his head no.

"It was after that argument I was no longer invited to the campouts. So I really miss you, Pascal. Things would be much better if you hadn't left me," said Philippe.

"I am so sorry to hear of your difficulties," said Pascal. "I just know some day you will become a great leader in the Brombey Forest, but my place is not here now. There is so much for me to learn, and I cannot learn it here. But I will come back to visit."

Then Pascal left the forest and returned to his school.

Some time later Pascal once again returned home. He found Philippe resting at home. "Hello Brother. I'm back to visit. Let's have a race."

Philippe stood, struggling a bit to get up on all fours.

"Wow! Yours are the biggest antlers I have ever seen. And again, it is not even yet the season for antlers. How do you do it?" Pascal asked.

Philippe frowned. "Welcome back, Pascal. There are many things I'd like to take credit for, but this is not one. These antlers are a curse. During the season for antlers they will grow even larger. Then, when it is time for them to fall off, only part of them will break off. And they just keep growing and growing."

"Maybe they will stop growing. When I go back to school I will see if I can find an answer. You know, I am in graduate school now. There are many bright animals there. I'm sure someone will have an answer," said Pascal.

"That would almost be worth you having left, Pascal," said Philippe.

Pascal jumped around and smiled. "Come on. Let's see how well you can run in those things."

"I don't know. They are quite heavy now."

"You are a great athlete," said Pascal. "Surely you must be able to carry such magnificent antlers with great speed and agility."

And with some encouragement Pascal got Philippe to race with him to the dead pine tree. But this time Pascal beat Philippe. And when Philippe got to the tree he was completely out of breath.

Once Philippe caught his breath he became angry. "I told you I did not want to race. Why did you make me do this? You have humiliated me. Isn't it enough that you abandoned me here? Now go away and leave me alone. I don't need any more troubles."

Pascal apologized and begged and pleaded with his brother. But it made no difference. Philippe would no longer talk with him. So Pascal left and went back to school. But before he left he said, "Philippe, you are a great athlete, and one day you will be a great leader."

Then one day Pascal received news that he should go home because his brother was sick and would die. So Pascal raced home as quickly as he could and went to see Philippe. What he saw astonished him. Philippe's antlers were enormous. They were larger even than the largest moose antlers. Philippe, now quite thin, was laying on the ground unable to move because of the great weight.

Pascal turned to Sam Smelly, a skunk and old friend of Pascal's, who was trying to take care of Philippe. "How is he? How did this happen?"

Sam looked up at Pascal. "I found him here like this. He can't move. I have done my best to feed him, but now he often refuses to eat."

Pascal turned to Philippe. "Brother, I am here. I will do what I can to help you."

Philippe opened his eyes. "Is that you, my brother who deserted me? Go away and let me die. You and all the other deer have abandoned me. Not a single deer has come to my aid. Not that any could help. Still, I hate them all."

"Brother, you are sick and speaking nonsense," replied Pascal. "I will get you some help." Then he turned to Sam. "Do what you can to make him eat and drink. I will be back as soon as I can."

Pascal went to look for help, but then he stopped. He didn't know what kind of help his brother needed. So he thought about it. Then he saw a family of chipmunks chewing on seeds and thought maybe they were the answer. "Chipmunks, can you please come with me. My brother, Philippe, is in desperate need of help."

"We know Philippe. He is a big, mean, and conceited deer. Why would we help him?" they asked.

"Please, if you will not do it for him, will you please do it for me? And if you will not do it for me, will you please do it just because it is the right thing to do?" Pascal asked.

"Okay, we will help if we can," replied the chipmunks.

So Pascal and the chipmunks went back to Philippe who was now asleep. Pascal asked the chipmunks, "With your sharp teeth can you please try to cut through his antlers?"

The chipmunks climbed all over Philippe's antlers and started biting. "Ow, this is hurting our little teeth, and we cannot cut into his antlers. They are too hard. We are sorry we cannot help."

"Well, thank you so much," said Pascal. "You were very nice to try."

"You are really quite welcome. We will bring him some sweet-smelling flowers. Maybe that will help him to feel better. He can enjoy them when he wakes up," they said.

Then the chipmunks left and Pascal went out still thinking this was the best way to attack the problem. Then he ran into a family of squirrels who were out playing. "Excuse me, I have a problem, and I think you might be able to help."

"We'd be happy to help. What do you think we can do for you?" they asked.

"Please, if you could, could you please try to cut through my brother Philippe's antlers?" asked Pascal.

"We know Philippe. He is mean and conceited. We would help anyone else. But we won't help him," the squirrels replied.

"If you won't do it for him, would you please do it for me? And if you won't do it for me, will you please do it because it is the right thing to do?" Pascal asked.

The squirrels chatted among themselves and then turned to Pascal. "Thank you, you are right. We should try to help."

So Pascal and the squirrels went to Philippe. The squirrels jumped all over Philippe's antlers and tried to chew through them. "Ouch, his antlers are like a rock. We can't cut through them. We are very sorry. We cannot help."

"Thank you very much for trying," said Pascal. "It was very kind of you."

"Please, when Philippe wakes up, can you please tell him we did it for him? We had forgotten that we should be kind to animals who are not kind to us. And we will bring him some shelled chestnuts. He should like to eat those when he gets well enough."

Pascal smiled. "Yes, of course. I'll let him know."

Pascal went back to searching for help. He heard what sounded like a great knocking in the trees. He looked up and spotted a large woodpecker. "Hello, Mr. Strongbeak, is that you? Could I please speak with you about a matter of some urgency?"

"Most certainly you can," said Mr. Strongbeak as he flew down to Pascal. "What seems to be the problem?"

"My brother Philippe is about to die because he cannot shed his huge antlers. They are so large he can no longer bear their weight. Do you think you might try to cut them off with your powerful beak?" asked Pascal.

"I have heard of Philippe. I am surprised he is your brother. You are so polite and I've heard he is quite conceited. Nevertheless, I'd be quite happy to try. I'll even bring along some other woodpeckers."

"That would be most kind of you," replied Pascal.

So Mr. Strongbeak got a few of his friends to come along, and they accompanied Pascal. They found Philippe still asleep but now with wonderfully scented flowers and shelled chestnuts close to his head.

The woodpeckers set to work. They made quite a noise as they repeatedly struck Philippe's antlers with their beaks. They hit them so hard that Philippe's body shook.

"We are very sorry, Pascal. We are afraid if we continue either we will break our beaks or we will turn Philippe's brain into mush. Maybe if you got someone with really big and sharp teeth it would work. You might talk with Mr. Broadtail down at the beaver pond. But we will bring some honey for Philippe. It is full of energy and might help him," said the woodpeckers.

"I am very grateful that you tried. Thank you ever so much," said Pascal.

"Don't give it a second thought. We are actually quite happy to help anyone we can," replied the woodpeckers.

So the woodpeckers flew off and Pascal went to find Mr. Broadtail at the beaver pond. He found him tending to his dam. "Mr. Broadtail, I wonder if I might have a word with you."

"Certainly. Certainly. Just one more good whack and this

branch will be in here solid." Mr. Broadtail then hit the mud next to a branch with his powerful tail. The sound echoed through the forest.

Mr. Broadtail lumbered over to Pascal on the bank of the pond. "I don't believe we have met before. I am Reginald Louis Broadtail III. And with whom do I have the pleasure of speaking?"

"My name is Pascal. I am the twin brother of Philippe," said Pascal.

"I am pleased to meet you, though I am glad you did not bring your twin with you. He is so arrogant and impolite," said Mr. Broadtail. "Do you know he claimed I had offended him by cutting down his favorite tree with which he scratched his back?"

"I am quite sorry he did that. And it is actually about Philippe that I have come," said Pascal. "He is in a terrible state. He will die if nothing can be done for him. His antlers have grown so large that they have pinned him to the ground. And they won't come off. The chipmunks, squirrels, and woodpeckers were all so very kind to try to bite and chip their way through them. I was very hopeful, that you might please try to help with your powerful, sharp teeth."

"I will do it, but only because you ask so nicely. I will do it for you," said Mr. Broadtail.

Mr. Broadtail and Pascal went to Philippe, and there Mr. Broadtail tried with all his might to cut through his antlers. Despite all the vibration Philippe hardly stirred.

"I have tried my best," said Mr. Broadtail. "I cannot try any harder. I am very sorry. And I am quite sorry to see Philippe in such bad condition. I am reminded we should be kind even to those who are not kind to us. Let me bring you some medicinal mud. I will put it on Philippe and it may help him to regain some of his strength."

"Thank you very much, Mr. Broadtail. You are so kind to

try and so kind to bring the medicine," said Pascal.

"Well, my boy, I don't know what you intend to do next, but I'm afraid his condition is quite serious. I would suggest you find Doctor Paws. He is the best doctor in these parts. He has a clinic where Farnhorn Creek and Brimhoffen Brook come together," said Mr. Broadtail.

"Thank you very, very much, Mr. Broadtail. I can never repay you for this," said Pascal.

"Don't give it a second thought," said Mr. Broadtail. "I am happy to do it, even for Philippe."

Pascal ran faster than he had ever run before and made it to the clinic very quickly. There he found Doctor Paws, an old, large brown bear, treating a duck with a broken wing. "I'm ever so sorry to bother you Doctor Paws, but this is an emergency."

Dr. Paws looked at Pascal over the top of his glasses. "You look quite fine to me. You can have a seat, and I'll get to you soon. I've just finished here with whom I thought to be my last patient for the day."

Then Dr. Paws turned to the duck. "Off you go now. I'll see you back in two weeks to check on your wing."

"Thank you very much," said the duck as he waddled away.

Dr. Paws then turned his attention to Pascal. "What seems to be the problem, young one? You look fine."

"Sir, it isn't me. It's my twin brother, Philippe. He is very ill and will likely soon die if something cannot be done for him. His antlers have grown so large he cannot bear their weight. They never fall off, and they just keep growing year after year. We've tried to bite and chip them off, but nothing has worked at all. Please, can you come right away? He is so sick he will not even wake up now."

"That indeed sounds like an emergency," said Doctor Paws. "We can go now. You just lead the way."

So Pascal and Dr. Paws went to see Philippe though at a much slower pace than Pascal would have preferred. But they made it, and there was Philippe now with Mr. Broadtail's mud on him. It must have done something for him, for now Philippe's eyes were open and Sam Smelly was feeding him some of the honey and chestnuts which the other animals had brought.

Philippe looked at Pascal. "Have you come to watch me die? You left me years ago and only came back to humiliate me when I started to become weak. And now you've come to pretend to care."

"That's not true Philippe," said Pascal.

At this point Sam Smelly stood on his hind legs and stared sternly at Philippe. "That is not true at all, you egotistical, ungrateful, moron. I found you here unable to move. I sent word for your brother and he came right away. And all this day he has been getting animals to come and try to free you from your gargantuan antlers. And the medicine on your neck and the food you are eating and the flowers you smell now are from those animals who tried to help you. And here he has brought the doctor. I tell you, if it weren't for your brother, I would turn around, let you have it, and leave you here to die."

"That would be just like a skunk, just to leave somebody to die," retorted Philippe.

Sam Smelly then turned to Pascal. "I am so sorry, but I cannot bear this. I am leaving." Then Sam Smelly, with tail lifted high, sauntered away.

Dr. Paws then turned to Pascal and motioned for him to follow. They walked out of earshot of Philippe. "You are right, Philippe will die soon. I doubt he even has more than a couple of days, though the mudpack Mr. Broadtail gave him has helped. But there is nothing I can do to help him. His fate is up to him."

Pascal looked puzzled. "What do you mean his fate is up to him?"

"Whether he lives or dies, it is up to him. There is only one animal I know of who can help your brother," said Dr. Paws.

"Who is it? I will go get him," said Pascal eagerly.

"It is the prophet," replied Dr. Paws.

"The prophet? How can a prophet help my brother?"

"By showing him the truth. Then it is up to your brother," said Dr. Paws.

Pascal stared at the doctor and bit his lower lip.

Dr. Paws saw Pascal did not understand. "Your brother does not have a medical problem. It is a problem of the soul which is manifested in a physical way. The creatures in this forest are by nature quite kind and forgiving. In all my years I've only seen two other cases of this. Your brother holds in himself years of unforgiveness that has grown as large as those antlers. And those antlers are as hard as his heart. That is why they will not come off. Now go to the top of Howler Hill and wait for the prophet. If you are lucky you will make it back here tomorrow morning with him."

"But how can I be sure I will find him?" asked Pascal.

"You can't. You just have to go and wait until he comes to you," answered Dr. Paws.

Pascal ran as quickly as he could two hills over to the top of Howler Hill. Then he ran back and forth calling out for the prophet until he became exceedingly tired. The sun had gone down and, try as he might, he could not keep his eyes open, and he fell asleep.

He awoke to hot breath in his face. "What have we here? This must be my midnight snack. Maybe I will ask who it is before I eat him."

Pascal opened his eyes and saw two glowing disks in a shadowy face directly in front of his face. Startled, he jumped to his hooves so as to run off. But a big paw with claws extended landed solidly and somewhat painfully on his back and kept him from running. "Here, here. Don't be so unfriendly. Let us have a little visit before I eat you."

"Please don't eat me. I came here to see if the prophet can help my brother. He's very ill," cried Pascal. "Do you know the prophet?"

"Oh bother, and here I thought I could eat you."

"You mean you won't eat me?" asked Pascal.

"No, I won't eat you."

"Do you know the prophet?" asked Pascal.

"I am the one you are seeking. Just what seems to be the problem with your brother that you think I can help?" asked the prophet.

So Pascal went on to explain what Dr. Paws had told him and the prophet agreed to try to help. Then the prophet told Pascal to stay for a few hours and get some sleep and that he would go on ahead to meet with his brother. For some reason this seemed like a good idea to Pascal and he fell quickly asleep.

When Pascal awoke it was already midmorning. He felt

the warmth of the sun on his body and thought how wonderful it was until he remembered his brother. Then he was off like a shot to get back to his brother.

When he arrived he saw a huge black jaguar sitting in front of his brother. Their eyes were locked and neither moved though his brother was drenched with sweat.

"Hello, Pascal," came a whisper behind him. "Back here in the bushes."

Pascal walked back toward the bushes and found Sam Smelly lying beneath them. "As bad as your brother has been to me, I couldn't stand to just leave him here. I got here at sunrise and found them like that. They haven't moved at all," whispered Sam. "Do you know who the cat is?"

Pascal laid down close to Sam. "I suppose he is the prophet that Dr. Paws mentioned yesterday. I went to get him yesterday but it was so dark when he arrived that I did not see him well at all. Dr. Paws said he is the only one who can help Philippe see the truth. Then, whether he lives or dies is up to Philippe."

Pascal and Sam then waited and watched in silence as the prophet and Philippe stared at each other. Then as late afternoon began to roll into evening Philippe's eyes began to fill with tears and there was a powerful crack that echoed like thunder and shook the ground. And Philippe's head came loose from the antlers. Then he began to sob.

The cat turned around and walked up to Pascal. "It is done. Your brother will live. Let him sleep as long as he needs." Then the cat turned and began to leave.

"Wait. Is that it?" asked Pascal. "I forgot to ask how much you are paid."

The cat turned his head back to Pascal. "Paid? No, I am not paid. The truth is plain to see. It is freely given. What you do with it. Well, that is the key."

Then without another word he was off, leaving Sam and

Pascal wondering what this all meant. But they had to wait until morning since Philippe now appeared to be fast asleep.

Pascal awoke the next morning at the prodding of Sam. "He's beginning to stir."

Pascal looked over at his brother who struggled to get to his hooves but then laid back down again. He looked over at Pascal. "It seems I'm not quite up to that just yet, but someone was kind enough to leave honey and chestnuts for me. They look delicious."

Philippe began eating what was left of the honey and chestnuts as Pascal and Sam got up and walked over to him. "How are you today," they asked.

"I am better than I have ever been. And I don't mean that in an arrogant sort of way. I mean I feel free. I feel free of an unbearable burden," said Philippe. "Won't you two please join me and have some honey and nuts?"

Pascal and Sam tried to politely decline thinking Philippe probably needed to eat all that was there, but he insisted so strongly that they accepted the invitation.

Philippe looked at Sam. "I am so sorry. I behaved so badly toward you, as well as everyone else. Please forgive me. You saved my life."

"I accept your apology, Philippe," said Sam.

Philippe then turned to Pascal. "Brother, I do not know where to begin with you. For the longest time I felt that you had abandoned me. And I treated you horribly. If you can forgive me for years of bad behavior, please do."

"It did hurt, Philippe. But I have never held it against you. Still, I forgive you," said Pascal.

"Thank you, Sam. Thank you, Pascal. I am so grateful for your forgiveness. Truly, it is a wonderful gift to me. It is sweeter even than this honey," said Philippe.

Then Sam looked at Philippe. "Philippe, what happened yesterday? What did that big cat do?"

Philippe paused and looked out in the distance and then back at Sam and Pascal. "I don't know. I woke up and there was a huge cat staring down at me. I thought that was it. I thought it was all over. But all he did was stare at me. And then my eyes met his, and I no longer saw him. Inside that gaze I saw the maker of my soul. And I cowered before him, unable to move, and unable to utter a sound. Then he showed me my every wrong thought, motive, word, and action. Everything I had done was laid out before me. I saw the darkness of my heart. Then I felt something I think I had never felt before. I felt sorry. I don't mean self-pity. I felt devastating regret for all the bad things I had done. And the wrongs others had done to me – if anyone has actually wronged me – they all disappeared. I felt so ashamed. And I asked for forgiveness. And he forgave me. Then there was morning, this wonderful, blessed morning. And I have joy and peace and thankfulness. And I am free of my burdensome antlers."

Pascal and Sam could see the change in Philippe. And over time they got to see this new Philippe was genuine. When he regained his strength he went to all the animals he had wronged and apologized to them. He became the most humble and generous deer in the forest and began to show a great deal of wisdom. In fact, the other deer were so impressed that they made him their leader. And though Philippe never again grew antlers, all the lady deer said he truly was the nicest, most decent, and most gentlemanly male deer in the forest.

OF TURTLES AND BIRDS

Twelve Ponds was the place to live. It was a large, luxurious habitat encompassing twelve expansive ponds well suited to the many turtles who called it home. Reginald Leach was well aware of the political importance of the area and was very proud to serve as its mayor. He was certain some day this would lead him on to bigger and better things in the turtle world.

But this election season was tough, really tough. Mayor Leach, who was married, had been through some scandalous times with some ladies and was locked in a tight political race against challenger Boxy Boxer, or BB for short.

Mayor Leach and BB met for the grand debate in front of the entire community. Turnout for the debate was quite impressive. That was either a good thing or a bad thing depending on how one felt he was doing. And Mayor Leach thought he was not performing well at all based on the laughter and boos when he appeared on stage.

But as it normally seemed to happen for the mayor, something fortuitous occurred. Patricia Paulson, a turtle who was always into the latest trends no matter how impractical, shouted out, "I want to be a bird. Mr. Mayor, if you are reelected will you change me into a bird?"

BB, who was normally quite thoughtful and slow to answer, made his first and last mistake by answering, "That's crazy. Turtles cannot become birds. Really, you must be serious."

Boos and muttering began to come from the crowd and grew quite loud. It was considered quite impolite to answer out of turn and to insult a turtle in the audience was unacceptable.

Mayor Leach saw this as his chance to score political points with the ladies, and he went for it all the way. "Why, Ma'am, let me apologize for my opponent's bad form. I'm sure if he had thought about it carefully, he would have answered you politely, indeed if he had answered at all, since you directed your question to me. Let me tell you, I think that is a wonderful, creative, and courageous idea. Why it's just the kind of thinking we need around here. I tell you, if you will accept it, I will hire you this very day to be in charge of changing all turtles who want to be birds into birds. And if I'm reelected I will make sure this program continues. You already know what will happen if you elect my challenger."

Cheering erupted from the crowd, and the mayor had Patricia come up on the stage and stand beside him.

The debate was over. Everyone had heard what they wanted to hear. BB simply sighed, turned around, and took his shell back home.

Mayor Leach won reelection easily after that. One would have thought the mayor would have tried to move away from the notion of turning turtles into birds. But he didn't. He saw how politically popular it could be, that it could bring in more money, and that it could launch him into bigger and better things.

So, Mayor Leach gladly worked with Patricia to come up with a strategy.

At the next community meeting, Mayor Leach and Patricia announced the first step in their grand vision. For the sake of the children, that the children could do more than any turtle had done before, they would train the baby turtles how to become birds. All it would take would be a slight tax increase to pay for the program, some turtle parents to give up their clutches of eggs, and some birds who would take the babies under their wings.

About half of the turtles were in favor and about half were against, but in the end it passed, and the community set about finding some willing birds. At first they talked with Raven because he was quite friendly with the turtles. But he told them they were crazy and flew away. So they put an ad in the community paper, and not long after that Owl showed up and told the mayor and Patricia that he would do the job for free. And off went Owl with several clutches of eggs.

Sometime later, Mayor Leach and Patricia, who had now become quite chummy, asked Owl how it was going and why they hadn't seen any of the babies.

Owl responded, "Oh, it's going quite well. I gave the eggs to other owl families. The baby turtles hatched and they all flew away."

"Well, why haven't we seen any of them?" asked Patricia.

Owl cocked his head to one side. "Of course you haven't. They are birds now. All of them became birds. They won't come back to you. You didn't say you wanted them to come back to you."

"Oh," sighed Patricia. "I hadn't thought about that."

"Well maybe next time, I mean if you would be so kind, perhaps you could tell them to come by and say hello to us," said the mayor.

Owl thought a bit. "Well, that seems fair. You bring us a

bunch of eggs and we'll make sure to have your babies say hello to you before they fly away."

Not too much later, the turtles had another community gathering. The mayor and Patricia updated them on the great success of the program. And then they said it was so successful that they needed many more eggs. So a number of the turtles gave up their clutches of eggs to the mayor and Patricia. But, of course, all the turtles had to keep paying the tax.

Some of the turtles complained, having seen no evidence of turtles that had become birds, but it had become such a popular program that there was nothing they could do about it. So at the appointed time, the turtles brought their eggs together and then Owl and his friends took them away.

Weeks later, Raven paid the mayor and Patricia a visit. "You are fools. Your babies are not becoming birds. Owl and his friends are eating them."

"Oh, I'm sure you're mistaken, Raven," replied the mayor.

"You're a fool, Leach. You're a total fool. And you too, Miss Patricia." Then Raven jumped into the air and flew away.

Mayor Leach and Patricia didn't believe Raven, but they thought it best to visit Owl anyway. So they went off and found Owl. They called up to him in his tree. "Mr. Owl, can you please come down here. We'd like to talk."

Mr. Owl flew down to a lower branch. "Yes, friends, what is it you want?"

"How's it going with the baby turtles?" asked the mayor.

"Oh, they all flew away. Don't tell me they didn't come by to say hello. We told them they must say hello."

"This is very disappointing," said the mayor.

"You know how children are," said Owl. "It's hard to get them to listen. Once they learn how to fly, that's all they want to do. But I must say, your babies are the best. They are very quick learners. Was there anything else? I need to get back to sleep so I can go to work tonight."

"Well, yes there was one thing," said the mayor. "We are so sorry to ask you."

"Raven told us you are eating our babies. Is this true?" blurted out Patricia.

"Stupid bird," muttered Owl. "He better watch out."

"What was that?" asked Patricia. "We couldn't quite hear you."

"There's no good way to put this, but I have to tell you, not all of your babies come out okay. Some have bad problems. And of course we have to eat those. You wouldn't want them to suffer would you?" said Owl staring down at them.

Mayor Leach kept silent thinking it best to let Patricia answer. It was much better politically to see what she thought and then to join in with her.

"No, I guess that is reasonable," replied Patricia. "How many do you think you have to eat?"

"No more than half a dozen. They had very bad problems. We really had no choice," said Owl, doing his best to seem sympathetic. "Is that all? I really do need to get back to bed."

"Would you be able to handle another bunch of our babies and let us know right away when they hatch?" asked Patricia.

"This is a bit of a bother," said Owl. "It really takes a lot of work. But I suppose, it does take a few days to teach them how to fly. You could come to visit them just when they hatch and maybe you could convince some to go back to live with you."

So Mayor Leach and Patricia were in for another batch of eggs. They told the turtles how successful the program was and how all their babies had learned very quickly how to fly and then had taken off to start turtle bird families elsewhere. Then they announced the need for more eggs so they could convince some of the new turtle birds to come and live with them. And once again the eggs were delivered to Owl and his friends.

The day after the delivery Raven came to talk with Mayor Leach and Patricia. "You fools. This very night Owl and his friends are going to have a party. They are going to eat all of your babies."

"That's not possible," sputtered the mayor. "Owl told us he only eats the sick ones."

"Come with me tonight, and you will see," replied Raven.

That night Raven led the two to Owl's party far away from the ponds. To their horror, there were Owl and his friends feasting on the turtle eggs.

Patricia started to let out a cry, but Raven stopped her. "If you cry out they will certainly try to eat me and they might try to eat both of you."

So they started back to Twelve Ponds. Behind them they could hear Owl saying how foolish the turtles had been to believe him and to believe that a turtle could ever become a bird. And all the other owls raised a wing and drank a toast to Owl.

Mayor Leach and Patricia decided they could never tell the turtles what had happened to their babies. At the next meeting they would say how they had visited with the babies and how beautiful their wings were but that they could not convince any to come and fly back to them.

The next meeting came and they did that and more. Mayor Leach, Patricia, and all of the mayor's staff came out with wings stuck to their shells.

The audience stood with their mouths agape.

Then Patricia stepped forward and announced, "All our dear babies became turtle birds and have flown away. We, however, cannot become turtle birds the same way. But we have learned the secret. We have become turtle birds."

Laughter began to break out and a turtle yelled from the audience, "You haven't become a bird. Those are just feathers stuck on your shells."

"We have so become birds. You're just not a believer, that's all," replied Patricia.

"If you're a bird then why don't you prove it by flying," retorted another turtle in the audience.

Patricia stammered trying to get some meaningful words to come out of her mouth.

The chant, "Fly. Fly. Fly," began to grow in the audience.

Mayor Leach saw this was going very bad, very quickly. He stepped up beside Patricia and addressed the audience. "Surely this learned audience is aware that not all birds fly."

At that all the turtles in the audience quieted down and began to nod at each other. "That's true. What the mayor said is true."

"Think of the penguin. It doesn't fly," said the mayor. "But it's a bird. Really, it's a bird and a fish. Part of the time it is a flightless bird and part of the time it is a fish. That's why it's called the penguin fish."

The mayor looked around at all the turtles in the audience. He could see enough of the turtles nodding their heads that none of the other turtles would dare challenge him on calling penguins, penguin fish.

"Now I tell you, this week we will start, for a slight fee, converting all turtles who want to become birds into turtle birds."

Applause broke out throughout the audience. The meeting was over and the turtles celebrated the creation of the turtle bird.

The mayor was very pleased with himself. Money had flowed in for the conversion of baby turtles to birds and now money was flowing in as more and more turtles decided they wanted to become turtle birds. Of course, as so often happened, some of that money flowed right into the mayor's personal coffers.

At the next meeting, most of the turtles arrived sporting their new feathers. But the deputy mayor had to start the meeting as the mayor was nowhere to be found. The deputy mayor started by excusing the mayor's absence and then by addressing the success of the turtle bird program. "Never, in the history of Twelve Ponds, have we ever seen something so radical and so successful. Truly, the vision of Mayor Leach and his exceptionally able assistant, Patricia, has enabled us to soar to new heights."

The turtles cheered at that but then suddenly became quiet and stared at the stage. The mayor and Patricia had just gotten on to the stage and were not wearing any feathers. You see the mayor and Patricia, who had become very chummy, had been expressing their chumminess, something you could not do wearing feathers. That expression had made them late for the meeting, and in their hurry they had completely forgotten about their feathers.

The deputy mayor walked over to them and quietly told them of their oversight. The mayor looked out at the audience staring at him and quickly made a bold decision.

"Fellow Twelve Ponders, Patricia and I are late because we have just made an important new discovery. You do not have to have feathers to be a turtle bird. Just think of the flying fish bird and the flying squirrel bird, not to mention the bat bird. None of them have feathers. And so we now know we do not have to have feathers to be turtle birds."

"But we all got feathers to be turtle birds," shouted a turtle from the audience.

"All that is well and good," replied the mayor. "If you want to have feathers you can have feathers. If you don't, then you don't have to."

"But we had to pay for these feathers," some in the audience said.

"And that is how it should be," replied the mayor. And then without a pause, he continued. "The money was in part necessary to make sure everyone was recorded properly as a turtle bird. So now, if you want to be a turtle bird – And I don't know why anyone would not want to be a turtle bird. – then you must pay a fee. But of course we can now lower the fee for registering as a turtle bird.

This seemed good to all in the audience. The meeting was over and the celebration began.

Life was now very good in Twelve Ponds. The mayor was secretly happy because his wife had died which had allowed him the political advantage of being the grieving widower and then the rescued widower as he and Patricia then had a public romance and a grand wedding.

And finally, all of the turtles who wanted to had become turtle birds. The mayor wasn't really happy about that as the registration of new turtle birds had brought in a lot of money. But the mayor's reputation had spread well beyond Twelve Ponds and he was now on the list for higher office. So he didn't care much about creating new schemes to make more money. He wasn't going to be there long.

Some time passed and once again the community had gathered. This was for a special occasion. It was the first annual celebration of the creation of the turtle bird. Everyone was in high spirits and the mayor had just concluded his opening remarks.

It was then that Raven flew down to the mayor. "I have a special important announcement."

"Go ahead and make it," said the mayor who had already had one too many.

"Good turtles of Twelve Ponds. I have an announcement of great importance. It has been reported, and I have seen with my own eyes, that the turtle flu is heading this direction. It is deadly. If you leave now, you may live."

"Why do we need to worry about that, Raven? You are out of your mind. We are turtle birds not turtles. The turtle flu will not hurt us," came the reply from the audience. "The turtle flu doesn't hurt birds. Just ask the mayor."

All eyes turned to the mayor. "Well, Leach, what are you going to do?" asked Raven. "Will you tell them the truth that a turtle cannot become a bird, or will you lie to them and let them all die?"

The mayor looked at Raven and then back to the audience. This was a quite unexpected turn of events. If he were to warn everyone then they would say he had lied to them. His chances for higher political office would be over. On the other hand, he thought, the turtle flu might not hit them.

"Raven, you are out of your mind just like these turtle birds said. Turtle flu will never hurt us. We are turtle birds," replied the mayor. "Now go. Fly away, and never come back. Your foolishness is not welcome here."

"You are the fool, Mayor," squawked Raven loudly. "You and all you turtle birds are fools. You are turtles and you will always be turtles. You cannot become a bird just by saying you are a bird. You will die, and see if I care."

Then Raven left and the turtles went about their merriment though some had listened to Raven and decided they would quietly leave Twelve Ponds for awhile.

Two months later Raven returned to Twelve Ponds or what was left of it. He could find nary a turtle, that is, nary a live turtle.

"Raven," came a strong familiar voice. "How good it is to see you."

Raven looked around and flew down to the ground. "BB, what are you doing here? I thought you would have left a long time ago and never returned."

"I did leave after that nonsense about turtle birds started," answered BB. But then I heard how badly Twelve Ponds was hit by the turtle flu. I wanted to see if there was anything I could do."

"Have you seen anyone you know?" Raven asked.

BB frowned and sighed. "Few of the turtles survived and I've seen very few I knew from before."

"What about the mayor and Patricia?" asked Raven.

"Dead," said BB. "I think Patricia really thought she was a bird. That mayor, though, I hear he found an excuse to leave. He said something about being called to the governor's office. But the night before he was to leave there was a bad flood. He got stuck here, caught the flu, and died."

"Serves him right," said Raven. "Because of him these turtles died. How could it have happened, BB?"

"I hate to say it, Raven, but sometimes turtles are as dumb as sheep. One sheep gets a dumb idea into its mind to do some fool thing and before you know it most of the sheep are doing the same fool thing" answered BB. "I don't suppose you would understand."

"Oh, I think I understand," Raven replied. "Sometimes we can do some really stupid things also."

"Well, in this case, Patricia was the sheep with the dumb idea. For whatever reason, being a turtle wasn't good enough for her. She should have known she was special just as she was, and she should have known turtles cannot be changed into birds. But she didn't, and she wanted someone, the mayor, to make it happen for her," said BB.

"What happened certainly wasn't all her fault, though," said Raven. "Mayor Leach had a lot to do with it."

"Oh, yes. That's very true. In fact, I don't blame Patricia. I think the turtle community needs a good shepherd. If the shepherd is good and wise then the community will tend to go that way. If the shepherd is bad and foolish then the community will tend to go that way," said BB.

"I think that is probably right," said Raven. "Bad and foolish - that was Leach for sure."

"Yes. That was Mayor Leach," said BB. "He was the turtle elected to watch over and protect the community. Patricia expressed her dream for more and better to be done for her by asking to be changed into a bird. Instead of commending her for her dream and talking about how, through hard work, we can accomplish great things, Mayor Leach exploited her. He didn't care about her or any other turtles. All he saw was an opportunity to gain more power and make more money. He didn't care about the consequences for the baby turtles or for the turtle community."

"What will you do now, BB?" asked Raven. "Will you be the good shepherd? I think you would be good."

"No, I'll do what I can to help rebuild the community. But that's it," answered BB. "I'm done with politics. While my heart may be in the right place, and I might not be corrupted by the position, I know I've lost the desire to suffer fools gladly. I knew that when I told Patricia she was out of her mind."

"It seems a shame," said Raven.

'No. It's okay." Then BB paused and looked at Raven. "It's just life. But I will hope and pray the Good Shepherd above will provide what is left of this community a good shepherd as they rebuild and grow."

And as it happened the Good Shepherd did provide a good shepherd for the turtles as they rebuilt their community. And BB and Raven continued on as friends even as they went on to other things.

The rain sent ripples across the surface of Bent Brook Pond. A lonely figure carrying a stick swam through the water to the beaver dam at the end of the pond and then disappeared under the water. He reappeared shortly thereafter without the stick. There, that ought to do it for awhile, he thought. It's time for dinner and to check on the missus. Then he disappeared under the water again.

Mr. Bartholomew Pugglesby was the co-creator and tender of the pond. He and his wife, Mrs. Penelope Pugglesby, had toiled long and hard to build the dam and the lodge in which they lived. They had to do it by themselves as they had settled in an area far away from other beaver. And now they were anxiously awaiting the birth of one or more kits.

Mr. Pugglesby made his way through one of the underwater entrances to their lodge. He climbed into the lodge, shook out his fur, and then walked over to his wife. "How's it going, Penny?"

"Anytime now. Anytime now," she said in a labored voice.

And she was right. Just two hours later one kit was born.

"All that work and only one was born. That just means you are all the more special," Mrs. Pugglesby said as she began to clean him.

"What will we call him?" Mrs. Pugglesby asked.

"I've always been partial to the name Emmett. It can mean strong worker. That is what a beaver needs to be," replied Mr. Pugglesby. "A beaver needs to be a strong reliable worker who takes joy in the reason God put him on this earth."

"That's sounds good to me," Mrs. Pugglesby replied. "Do you hear that, Emmy? You're going to be a strong worker."

"Now, Penny. I said Emmett, not Emmy."

"I know. But look at those cute little eyes and that precious nose. He has to grow into being Emmett," Mrs. Pugglesby answered.

Mr. Pugglesby looked at his son. "I think you have a point there, Penny. You're right. He does have to grow into it."

Emmett grew quickly, as beavers do, and not much more than a month had passed before his father and mother began teaching him everything he would need to know to take care of himself and his wife and family in the future.

They took him all over the pond and through all of the canals. "Emmett, we always have to keep these canals clear so we can travel safely and carry branches and food back to the dam and lodge. You never know when a bear or a wolverine may sneak up on you and attack you. You always want to stay in or close to the water."

They also taught him how to slap the water with his tale. "If you make this sound, then we will come find you. If you hear this sound, then you know something is wrong. You should respond and then make sure you are safe. Then you need to come find us."

And they showed him all types of trees. "Emmett, this type of tree is the best for food. This type of tree is very good for building the dam and keeping it strong."

Then they showed him a tree in one area not far from the lodge. "Emmett, this tree is very special. It is big and strong and very tall. You must never chew on this tree. If you cut it down it would probably fall on the lodge and maybe even destroy the dam."

His mom and dad took him to other places to show him where to get rocks and mud. Then they showed him how to use them to make the dam stronger. Time and again they would tell him, "Emmett, you must learn to listen to the water. You always need to listen to it. It makes a certain sound. When it changes you know there is a problem with the dam. You must swim out right away to fix it."

Emmett would always reply, "I don't hear it. All I hear is water moving. Moving water sounds like moving water. How am I supposed to be able to tell when there is a problem?"

They always responded, "Be patient. You will learn. Just listen. Always be listening. In time you will notice what is normal and what is not normal."

One day, when Emmett was ten months old, Mr. Pugglesby, noticing his son seemed to not be learning too well, sat him down and talked with him. "Emmett, someday, not too long from now, we will trust you to do things on your own. You will need to work very hard."

"But Dad, I am still so young. I need to go out and play. I don't want to be doing all this work. It is boring. All we do is work, work, work."

"Now, Son, you know that is not true," his father replied. "Didn't we wrestle in the mud just the other day?"

Emmett frowned. "I guess so."

"And didn't we play tug of war with a stick just yesterday?"

"Yes."

"So you see, we do play, but work must always come first."

"Why?" Emmett whined. "Why do we always need to work so much?"

"In time you will realize that a beaver is very special. God put us here for a very special purpose. We do something no other animal can do. We build wonderful strong dams. We provide homes and fresh water for many plants and animals. If a dam breaks, many animals will lose their homes and their water supply. We have a huge responsibility. Many animals rely on us. You need to be responsible and grow into your name. You need to be a strong worker. Then one day you can look out on your own pond and know that you have truly done something wonderful."

"Aw, but this is really hard. It's too hard. Maybe times have changed," replied Emmett.

"Emmett, I need to know if you will be a strong and responsible worker," his father said sternly. "Will you be strong and responsible?"

Emmett looked at his dad and squirmed. "All right, I can be strong and responsible. Can I go now?"

"Yes, but you must be back for dinner," Mr. Pugglesby answered as Emmett dove from the lodge into the water.

Mrs. Pugglesby, who had not been far away, walked over to her husband. "Dear, you know Emmy is still young. He will learn. He will grow up to be a responsible and strong worker. We just need to give him time."

"Penny, I wish I could agree with you. In a couple months he'll need to start going out to work by himself. We've taught him almost everything we know. He's shown no interest in what we do. If, after he's a year old, he isn't able to do the jobs we give him on his own then we really need to think about having him move out. I know normally he would be with us for a couple of years before he moves out, but we can't afford an extra mouth to feed when that mouth doesn't contribute to the family. Besides, it may be the only way he can learn is to go out on his own."

"No, Little Emmy isn't ready to start his own pond," cried Mrs. Pugglesby. "You can't be that cruel to him."

"I know if we kick him out soon after he's turned one that things will be tough for him. But it isn't cruelty, and you know it, Penny. It is a fact of life for beavers." Then Mr. Pugglesby looked his wife in the eyes. "And you need to stop calling him Emmy. He must realize it is time for him to grow up."

Mrs. Pugglesby sniffed and turned away from her husband. "I know you are right. I will call him Emmett. But please give him some more time. Not every beaver learns as quickly as another. And you know I am pregnant now. We may need extra help after I give birth."

"Yes, Penny. I will wait until after you give birth. That will give him time to prove himself," said Mr. Pugglesby in a softer tone. "And we will talk with him about it so it won't be a surprise to him."

After that the Pugglesbys gave Emmett simple jobs to go out and do on his own. At first he did very well. Then one day they sent him out to cut down some young saplings and bring them back to be stored by the lodge for food. But he didn't come back by the time Mr. Pugglesby returned to the lodge for dinner.

"Bart, have you seen Emmett?" asked Mrs. Pugglesby.

"No. I've been working on the dam, and I haven't seen him since we sent him out to get saplings. I figured he had already come home," replied Mr. Pugglesby. "Did you see him at all?"

"No. I haven't seen him since we sent him out. I do hope he is okay," Mrs. Pugglesby said, her eyes wide with fear.

"Don't you worry, Penny. I'll go look for him," said Mr. Pugglesby. "I'm sure he can't be too far."

Mr. Pugglesby dove out of the lodge and surfaced outside. There he slapped the water hard several times with his tale. The sound echoed through the entire valley.

Mr. Pugglesby listened hard for a response. Hearing none he set off to cover every nook and cranny in the pond and every canal they had built. He searched and searched but did not find his son. Surely, he must have gone home by now, he thought.

He turned back toward the lodge, anxiety gripping his heart as he neared it. He dove under the water and came up into the lodge.

"Bartholomew, did you find him? Is he okay?" Mrs. Pugglesby asked.

"Oh, Penny, I searched everywhere. I could find no trace of him," he said as he embraced his wife.

"Whatever could have happened to him?" she asked, tears in her eyes. "Maybe he was killed and dragged off and eaten."

"Don't go thinking that, Penny. It's still too soon. And I saw no sign of trouble anywhere. He'll show up," Mr. Pugglesby said.

"You must be exhausted," said Mrs. Pugglesby. "Let me get you some food."

Mr. Pugglesby yawned. "Don't bother. I'm just fine. I just need to relax."

Then Mr. Pugglesby closed his eyes and fell fast asleep.

It was around breakfast time when the silence was interrupted by splashing as Emmett entered the lodge. Mrs. Pugglesby, who, being so filled with worry for her son hadn't slept for a minute, ran over to him.

"Oh, Emmy, Emmy, Emmy. Are you okay? Are you hurt? Let me get a good look at you. Bartholomew, Emmy is back," Mrs. Pugglesby exclaimed as she examined her son closely.

Mr. Pugglesby woke with a start from a deep sleep and saw his wife and son. "Is it a dream? Is it really you, Emmett? Are you okay? What happened?"

"I'm sorry I'm so late," Emmett replied. "I was trapped in a canal by a bear. There was no way I could get home. The bear just sat there and waited for me. It finally got tired and left. Oh, I am so exhausted! I'm so sorry I couldn't get the food."

"Oh, Emmy, we're just glad you're safe," Mrs. Pugglesby replied as she comforted her son. "Sometimes bears will do that and you just have to wait."

"Emmett, that was very brave of you," said Mr. Pugglesby. "You did the right thing. Where were you? I searched everywhere for you. I searched all the canals and could not find you."

Emmett looked at his parents. "Well, uh, I'm actually quite embarrassed to say. You see, I really went quite far out. And I saw some good saplings away from the water. Everything looked clear. So I got out of the canal and walked quite a ways. I know I walked too far from the canal. And that's where the bear found me. It came after me and I had to hide in a bunch of thick brush until it got tired and left. I'm really sorry. I know I was supposed to stay by the canals. But those saplings looked so good."

"Yes, that was very foolish," Mr. Pugglesby said sternly. "But the important thing is that you're okay. And, I bet that is a lesson you'll never forget."

"Thanks, Dad."

"Are you okay? Did the bear hurt you?" asked Mr. Pugglesby.

Emmett yawned. "It came close, but it didn't get a paw on me. I never knew I could move that fast. Oh, I'm so tired."

The Pugglesbys let their son rest that day. The next day Mr. Pugglesby went with his son to gather some food. As they were swimming along, a young otter darted up to them. "Hey, Em. Boy did we have fun. When can you come and play again?"

Mr. Pugglesby turned and looked at the otter. "Emmett has work to do. You need to leave."

"Well, who made you the ruler of the pond?" the otter asked before darting off.

Mr. Pugglesby yelled after him. "You wouldn't have this pond to fish and play in, if it weren't for us. And we have to work to keep it in good shape."

Emmet looked at his dad. "Gee, he must be mistaken. I don't know him at all."

Mr. Pugglesby frowned. "There never was a bear was there, Emmett? You were off playing with that young otter weren't you?"

"No, Dad. Honest. He was mistaken," Emmett said.

"Don't lie to me, Emmett," Mr. Pugglesby replied. "How many times have I told you that you should never play with otters? Their lives are totally different. We have to work hard. They get to play a lot. And they are very mischievous. They are forever digging holes in the dam whenever they come around."

Mr. Pugglesby continued. "Emmett. Son. We were very worried when you did not show up. I got home and we discovered you were missing. I went right back out and looked for you. I looked everywhere. When you got back home we were so relieved. But now I know you were lying to us. You were doing so well. You were really helping us out by doing those small jobs we were giving you. And you don't realize how much you were helping yourself by doing them. What happened that you would do this?"

"You always make me work. I just don't see the point. I don't have enough time to play. And besides you're the one who moved way out here where there are no other beaver to play with. What did you expect me to do?" Emmett asked.

"I expect you to do your job. You are actually getting close to the age where you could be out on your own," replied Mr. Pugglesby.

"That would be just fine with you, wouldn't it, Dad?" Emmett said as he swam away.

Later, when Mr. Pugglesby returned home, he was met by his wife. "Please don't be too hard on Emmy. He's still just a boy. He's still learning to be responsible, and you do make him work a lot. Maybe we are pushing him too much. What do you think?"

"Penny, stop calling him Emmy. He isn't too young, and we aren't too hard on him. He has to grow up. As soon as our next kit or kits are old enough he will have to leave," replied Mr. Pugglesby.

"But, Bart…" Mrs. Pugglesby started to say.

"No. That's it. We will talk of this no more. He will never grow up unless we kick him out," Mr. Pugglesby growled as he shuffled off to go to sleep.

Mrs. Pugglesby followed her husband off to bed. "Bartholomew, I know you are right. It's just been difficult for me. What do you think we should do?"

"Let's sit down with the boy tomorrow and let him know he will have to go out on his own if he doesn't improve," said Mr. Pugglesby. "But, Penny, he didn't just goof off. He didn't just disobey us. He lied to us. If he decides to work hard, it's still going to be hard to trust him."

Mrs. Pugglesby sighed. "You're right."

The next day Mr. and Mrs. Pugglesby sat their son down and talked with him. And it went about as well as could be expected, which was not well at all.

Emmett's last words as he slipped out of the lodge were, "Well, now I know for sure you do not love me. I doubt you ever did love me." But he returned later in the day and, without saying anything to the contrary, began to help his parents with the things they asked him to do.

Not long after that the time came for Mrs. Pugglesby to give birth. There was much excitement in the lodge on that day as Mrs. Pugglesby gave birth to healthy twin girls. "Oh, aren't they beautiful?" Mrs. Pugglesby said to her husband. "Aren't they just the most adorable things you've ever seen? What shall we call them?"

Mr. Pugglesby looked at his twin girls and his heart filled with warmth. "I don't know, Penny. I don't think I want to try to name kids for what I want them to become any more. What do you think?"

"I've always loved the name Rosella. That was my great grandmother's name. And I've always liked the name Maricella," Mrs. Pugglesby said. "What do you think?"

"I think that sounds great. The first will be Rosella and the second will be Maricella." Then Mr. Pugglesby smiled and laughed. "And of course, we will call them Rose and Mari."

Mrs. Pugglesby then stayed at the lodge to take care of the two girls and Mr. Pugglesby did his best to work with

Emmett. But he never had Emmett do anything important because he no longer trusted his son.

Then one day Emmett returned home without his father. Mrs. Pugglesby asked, "Where is your father? He should be home by now."

Emmett looked at his mom with the twin girls. "I don't know. He went off by himself. He said something about getting some special mud somewhere. He doesn't have me do anything."

"Don't talk about your father that way. If you would just be responsible your father would trust you to do many things," Mrs. Pugglesby replied.

Emmett glared at his mom. "You don't care about me either. You just care about those girls."

Mrs. Pugglesby was going to respond but just then she saw Mr. Pugglesby poke his head into the lodge. She ran over to him. "Bartholomew, what is wrong?"

"I got tore up a bit by a wolverine, Penny," he said weakly. "Can you help me up?"

Mrs. Pugglesby grabbed her husband and pulled him in to the lodge. "Oh dear. That looks pretty bad."

"I'm afraid so, dear. But at least it's pretty much stopped bleeding. I just need to rest a bit," he said as he fell asleep right where he was.

Mrs. Pugglesby let him alone. She knew only time would heal his wounds. The next day he was still sound asleep, but she knew work needed to be done.

Mrs. Pugglesby looked at her son. "Emmett, I need you to…" Then she stopped. She knew even in this situation she could not trust her son to get work done by himself. "Emmett stay here with your sisters. You can take them outside of the lodge, but you must not go far at all. It is still too dangerous for them." Then she was off like a shot to go to work.

That was a long week for Mrs. Pugglesby. She worked very hard and she worried about her husband. He got worse the first few days but then started to get better. She was happy to see that and was greatly encouraged that Emmett seemed to be taking his responsibility for the girls seriously.

At the end of the week they sat down together for a meal. Mr. Pugglesby was still too weak to leave the lodge, but he looked much better. "How has it been, Penny?"

"It has been fine. It's been good to get back out and work hard. And I got everything ready for today," she said.

"What will happen today?" he asked.

Mrs. Pugglesby smiled. "There's going to be a big storm with a lot of wind and rain. You can hear it and smell it in the water and the air. And, of course, it has already started. And it may last for awhile. But we have plenty of food.

"That's good. That's good," Mr. Pugglesby said, nodding his head. Then he looked over at the girls. "And what have you girls been doing this week?"

"Emmy has taken us out each day. And he showed us a great tree to sharpen our teeth on. See, aren't our teeth sharp?" the girls said showing off their teeth to their parents. "He even made it a contest to see how fast we can cut it down."

"Yes, that's wonderful girls. That sounds like a lot of fun," Mrs. Pugglesby said. "I hope it isn't too far from the lodge though. You girls need to be careful. Emmett, you did keep them close didn't you?"

Emmett started to answer, but the girls interrupted him. "Oh, it is very close. It's that really really big tree that stands over our lodge. You should see it now. We've almost cut it down. A couple more days and we'll have that thing on the ground."

Mrs. Pugglesby looked at Emmett in disbelief. "Emmett, you haven't been having them work on the big tree have you?

We told you to never touch that tree. If it falls it will likely destroy the lodge and the dam."

Emmett squirmed. "What did you expect me to do? You told me to keep them close to the lodge, and all they want to do is cut wood. What else could I do?"

Mr. and Mrs. Pugglesby looked at each other. "Mr. Pugglesby said quietly and calmly, "Penelope, take the girls and Emmett now. I'm still too weak to go. I will stay here."

Mrs. Pugglesby's heart sank. She knew her husband was right. "Okay girls, we're going to go on an adventure right now."

"Oh, goody," the girls replied. "Let's go."

"You need to go too, Emmett. You can help me with the girls."

"Mom, I don't want to go. Nothing is going to happen. Even if that stupid tree falls, it won't fall on us. And the weather outside is going to be bad. It's much safer in here," Emmett said as he moved to the other end of the lodge.

"Go, Penelope. Go now. I will pray for you, and you can pray for us," said Mr. Pugglesby softly.

Mrs. Pugglesby hardened her resolve and then took off with the girls right behind her. She led them away from the lodge as quickly as she could and took them to a place where she believed they would not be swept away should the dam break. There they waited as the storm raged.

Then she heard it and felt it. A loud crack, a slow moan, and a thunderous crash which shook the earth. She knew the great tree had fallen. And the sound of the water told her the dam had been breached. But she stayed with the girls and waited for the storm to calm.

It seemed like an eternity to Mrs. Pugglesby, but finally the storm went away. She took the girls and headed back to the lodge. Where there was once a great pond there was now just a swollen creek. And where there had once been a grand lodge there was now a pile of branches.

Mrs. Pugglesby looked anxiously at the lodge, and her heart sank. Surely her husband and son had been lost. Nevertheless she clambered all over the pile to look. Then a small voice came from inside, "Penny, is that you? Did you and the girls survive?"

Mrs. Pugglesby heart raced as she recognized her husband's voice. "Yes, dear. We survived. We are here. We will get you out." So Mrs. Pugglesby and her daughters cut into the pile, and a very weak but whole Mr. Pugglesby emerged.

After some time Mr. Pugglesby's health was restored. He and Mrs. Pugglesby and their twin daughters worked hard building a new dam and lodge. And the daughters grew up, as Mr. Pugglesby thought all beavers should, to be hard working and responsible.

As for Emmett, no one knows what happened to him. The Pugglesbys always hoped he had been swept far away and was still alive. They felt sure he would then have become a very responsible and hard-working beaver who recognized his very special role in the world.

For, as Mr. Pugglesby knew, and even Mrs. Pugglesby would have to admit, if a beaver does not work hard, he will not long live. And there is joy and happiness for a beaver in fulfilling his purpose in life.

THE PROBLEM OF HANAMEEL MERCEDES

Many years ago, in a foreign country, there was a town called Mann. Now it was a bit of a snobbish town. They were happy, if you could call it happiness, with the way things were. And they weren't so accepting of outsiders.

One day a woman by the name of Hanameel Mercedes, known as Hana or, more commonly, "that woman," came to live there. About her there was no small amount of controversy. Everyone agreed, at least in their heart of hearts, that she was exceptionally gifted. But it was one expression of that gift, her great beauty, which earned her both praise and condemnation.

The women looked at her and feared for their husbands and boyfriends. If a woman walking with her husband were to see Hana coming toward them, she would quickly maneuver her husband in some other direction. This resulted in not a small number of accidents as a wife would push or pull her husband into the street or perhaps into a shop window to avoid her. But thankfully most of the injuries were minor scrapes and bruises.

When the women in the beauty parlor or the store would see Hana passing by, they would say, "She has no right to look like that. Here we have to work so hard to look our best. She does nothing, yet not one hair is out of place. Her face is perfect, and you can't even tell if she wears makeup."

"Her figure is perfect," another lady, Mrs. VanHoost, the town's grocery store owner and frequent visitor to the beauty parlor, would say. "And you know she does nothing to make it that way. She eats what she wants. Look at me. I eat one little chocolate and put on ten pounds." At that everyone would nod in agreement and comment that it was the same for them.

Other women would say, "She's always so nice too. Never a swear word. Never a harsh word." But then they would follow up with, "No one can be that good. She must be hiding something. Mark my words, there's something wrong with her."

"I can add to that," another lady would say. "You know how she spends all her time at the mission where all the bums go. So many of them are men. I bet she's the reason we've seen so many more of them coming to this town. Why if she weren't here, all the bums would go away and the mission would close. And we wouldn't have to be bothered by them anymore."

It didn't matter that so very very little of what they said was true. Once a woman made up a story about Hana, she and others began to believe it. Then they spread it to as many other ladies as they could. And they would go even further.

"Did you know she's having affairs with half the husbands in this town? Why I know for a fact she's having an affair with Hilda's husband, Hans. How do I know? My friend Anna told me that Hilda told her that Hans admitted to it."

While the women could be blamed for spreading false and malicious gossip about Hana, some of the falsehoods were, at least as far as they knew, true. You see some of the married men were so taken by Hana that they did claim to be having an affair with her. They weren't, but when it came down to looking bad in the eyes of their wives or not besting another man, they would rather have looked bad, very bad, to their wives.

A number of men, even those who were married, approached Hana and tried to gain her affections. To the married men she would say, "I know you must be temporarily out of your mind. I am sure you are a man of good character who would never want to do something so hurtful to your wife." Then she would say, "I pray you and your wife will be blessed," and walk away.

To the single men who approached her she would say, "My heart is for the people who need me and for those who share my heart for others. You don't recognize your true need for me, nor do you share my heart for those who do. You just want me because you think I am beautiful. But as soon as you would have me, you would decide I am, at best, a woman of average looks, if not just downright ugly. And then you would despise me. No, I am not what you are looking for."

The men would try to convince her of the sincerity and purity of their intentions, but she would have none of it. She would ask them, "Do you see the beauty in those broken people whom I spend my life serving? Do you see how you are like them?" And the men would answer, "No. Can't you see I am much better than they are? That's why you should love me. I have no such ugliness, and I have no such needs. With you as my wife there would be nothing I could not do, and you would never have to be bothered by such people again."

She then would reply, "It is as I said. You don't see your need for me, and you don't share my heart for those who do. No, you don't want me." The men would then depart from her presence, forlorn and greatly disappointed.

Some time passed and then something quite unforeseen happened. There was an announcement in the newspaper. Hanameel Mercedes was to be wed, and the entire town was invited to the wedding.

The women were excited and rejoiced. At last, she would no longer be a threat. And who knows, maybe she would no longer be so attractive. Let her see if she could keep her looks through having and raising kids. Or, even better, perhaps her husband was from another town and she would leave. They were absolutely giddy at the thought. Then they imagined what her husband would look like. Surely he would be incredibly handsome and a man of means. All the women decided they must go.

The men reacted quite differently to the news. How could they stand to see the most beautiful woman ever be married? Still, they thought, how could they not see the man who was able to catch such an unobtainable prize. So they also decided they must go. And those who were married or had girlfriends, if by chance they did not want to go, had no choice. All the wives and girlfriends demanded they go so they could experience the great disappointment of their men.

All this meant that on the day of the wedding the town filled the church to overflowing. Not a pew had empty space left, and not a few people had to stand. The fact that every pew was filled was made all the more amazing by the nature of some of those in attendance. Vagrants, male and female, who frequented the mission had come, shall we say, just as they were, fragrance and all. This caused no small amount of chagrin on the part of those from "proper" society. But in the end, this was just too good to miss. So there they all were like sardines in a can.

Finally, the music started and out stepped the groom. Those from the mission cheered and applauded while, from everyone else, there was an audible gasp. Men and women alike looked at the groom in disbelief. There stood a man they had seen for years wandering aimlessly on the street asking passersby for money. He stood in a well-worn, cheap, ill-fitted suit with a red carnation stuck in the buttonhole of his suit's lapel.

The mouths of all the men who had desired Hana so fervently hung open. They sat as in a stupor. For a moment there was no thought in their minds. They just sat and stared. But then their brains began to work again, and thoughts like, "How?" and "Why?" flooded into their minds.

Likewise, the mouths of the women hung open in disbelief as they began to look at each other. They made no sound, but each understood the other just by the facial expression – "Are you kidding?"

Now the women recovered much more quickly than the men, and soon they were whispering to each other, "It doesn't matter. She will be married and she will no longer be a problem. Besides we knew there was something wrong with her. This just proves it."

Then the wedding march began to play. The women with husbands and boyfriends prodded and shook their men back into reality, and then all stood and turned toward the back of the church.

The bride entered. Whether she was accompanied or not no one could recall, such was her great beauty. It filled the church and set every face aglow. They all stood transfixed following her with their eyes as she walked toward her groom. And then she stood next to him.

The contrast was stark. There stood side-by-side life and death, health and disease, perfection and corruption. The spell which had fallen on the people broke as they looked upon the true nature of the groom. The women mocked the bride in their hearts, "Surely, she has chosen foolishly. There is no future in this marriage. But at least we will be rid of her." The men wondered how they could ever have found her attractive. "I must have been out of my mind. She's got to be nuts. I'm much better looking than that trash."

They had these thoughts throughout the ceremony, so much so, that they heard none of the words. Some frowned and some sneered. Some even laughed out loud. But just as they did not hear the ceremony, so the bride and groom were equally oblivious of those in the audience. They gazed upon each other and heard only the words of the minister and of each other.

Then the time came as it does in so many marriage ceremonies for the bride and groom to kiss. And it was here, as the groom received the bride as his, that something quite extraordinary happened and one must wonder if it will ever happen again.

They kissed, and the groom was transformed. He was still the same person, but his countenance began to shine like that of the bride's. And his obviously second-hand clothes, which had not fit, became the finest and whitest tailored tuxedo, now with a white rose replacing the red carnation.

The people in the audience looked in awe at the bride and

groom. Those who had mocked and laughed were once again transfixed. They had never seen a finer couple. They wondered how this could be. At least the bride had always seemed special, but this man, this lowly creature, was laughable and detestable.

The men and women from the mission cheered loudly, breaking the spell which had fallen upon the town's people. They looked around in silence and then noticed something. It began to dawn on them that the bums from the mission were dressed in fine clothes and their faces shown like those of the bride and groom. This too amazed them, and they looked at each other to communicate their question, "How can this be?" But instead of seeing each other in their finery they saw they were now dressed in rags. Perhaps for the first time they saw themselves as they truly were. Horrified and ashamed, they fled to their homes and locked their doors.

The next day came and the people arose from their sleep. With trepidation, they glanced at themselves in their mirrors. What horror would await them? They looked once, then twice, and then a third time more carefully. To their great relief they found their appearance was back to normal. There was no ugliness. There were no raggedy clothes. All was back to what it should be.

So they stepped outside and went about their business, most not perceiving the grayness which now covered the town. If one were to mention it another would say, "Oh, really? I hadn't noticed. But even if it is, it's like a warm blanket. Don't you think?"

After a couple of weeks of not seeing Hana about town, the people began to believe she had left. No one had wanted to speak about what had happened at the wedding, how they had seen themselves as ugly and in rags. The experience was too horrifying. Each person thought, or perhaps more accurately hoped, it had been a delusion or a bad dream. And they thought perhaps no one else had experienced it. Each thought how horrible it would be if they had actually seen the truth. They wondered if they were, and feared that they might, be as bad off as they perceived the beggars to be.

So, they did not speak of the wedding but only talked about Hana being gone. The women were happy at the absence of the troublesome woman. The men were sad that such a prize to be possessed had disappeared.

Weeks went by before anyone noticed the mission was vacant. It was on the outskirts of town and was not near to anything essential. So, they had no reason to go by it. Its absence was considered no great loss. And, they thought, the bums might come back if they were to talk about it. Better to be silent on the matter.

Over time the memory of Hana faded. No one really wanted to remember her. Her presence had always been uncomfortable. Life was so much better to be lived without her.

The people never realized the gift that Hana was. In a way she was a bother. You either had to accept the gift that she was or reject her. You could not live in her presence without seeing your own imperfections. You could not possess her as a man possesses a trophy. You could not buy her. You could only receive her by admitting your poverty. And if you received her, you had to accept that you could not change her, but that she would transform you.

So, this little town went on never realizing the gift which had come to them. They never realized grace and mercy had been offered to them. For that is who Hanameel Mercedes was and what her name meant, the grace and mercy that comes from God. And all those who refused to admit their poverty had turned her away, tried to change her, or had tried to take her on their own terms.

Instead of accepting what they needed, they were given

what they wanted—a life without grace and mercy—which as it turns out, is no life at all. Things without life do not grow. And so, as it happens, little by little the town of Mann became smaller and smaller until all that was left was nothing at all.

Tis the end of this sad and woeful tale
Of wonderful life which was rejected
And the death which then silently befell.

But do not be despondent and so pale.
Great hope waits for you tis written and said
Only for you to so freely avail.

For God our Father despite the travail,
For the world He so loved and created,
Gave Jesus His son with no parallel.

He died for our sins and rose to prevail,
That all whom in Him believed and trusted,
Would receive life fore'er and with Him dwell.

Seeing God's grace and mercy don't rebel.
Don't bargain, buy, bribe, or be dejected.
Do not laugh at it, nor despise, nor rail.

Take it, freely offered and not for sale.
Receive it as it is to be granted,
Resplendent life at the end of the trail.